Other MHP Books By and With

Edward Lee:

- The Television
- The Bighead
- Czech Extreme

Madness Heart Press
2006 Idlewilde Run Dr.
Austin, Texas 78744

This is a work of fiction. Names, characters, places, and incidents either are the product of the author's imagination or are used fictitiously. Any resemblance to actual persons, living or dead, events, or locales is entirely coincidental.

Copyright © Edwatd Lee 2022

All rights reserved. No part of this book may be reproduced or used in any manner without written permission of the copyright owner except for the use of quotations in a book review. For more information, address: john@madnessheart.press

A MHP Pocket Book
www.madnessheart.press

The Bounce House

by Edward Lee

A Madness Heart Press Pocket Book

Thirty-five-year-old Miles Bennell, whom one could say fit the mold of tall, dark, handsome, and a bit of a sexist pig, watched out the front kitchen window as the workmen from the party-equipment company rolled the deflated bounce house off the truck and centered it neatly in the front yard.

Miles's wife, Becky, fragrant from just having showered, came out, looked out the window, and immediately complained, "Oh, Miles, tell them to put it in the backyard! In the front, it will look *ostentatious.*"

"That's the idea, honey." He quickly eyed the curve of her buttocks. *God-DAMN, she's got an ass on her that won't quit, even after eight years of marriage …* "Ostentatious—what's that mean? Snobby, right?"

Becky tossed back her dark blond jaw-length bob. "Yes, Miles. The neighbors will consider this a vulgar display of materialism and one-upmanship. Just like with the Christmas lights last year and our Halloween decorations. They'll think we're showing off." She shook her head, still looking out the window. "Don't we have more character than to Keep Up With

The Joneses?"

"Fuck the Joneses. I'll *bury* the Joneses—they can eat my shorts. We're *better* than the fuckin' Joneses, for fuck's sake," Miles replied with some striking disdain. Then he glanced aside and cupped Becky's right butt-cheek until she jiggled away. "All these asshole neighbors? They need to know that when *my* kid has a birthday, he gets the best of everything—including the best and biggest bounce house available." He smiled out the window. "I mean, look at the size of that thing; it's twenty-five by twenty-five and fifteen feet high; they don't even *make* residential bounce houses bigger than that. You could fit twenty *adults* in there, much less twenty eight-year-olds."

"Yes, and it's twice as big as the one the Grangers rented for their twins—that's my point. It looks like we're doing it on purpose, just to show them up. 'Our bounce house is bigger than yours.'"

"Yeah," Miles said. "Perfect. The fuckin' Grangers *wish* they had our money."

Becky could only smirk because she knew the futility of arguing with Miles. She looked closer out at the bounce house. "It must've cost a fortune," she muttered.

Miles couldn't resist. "No, what cost a fortune was your brand-new Cadillac V-Series Blackwing." *Ninety fuckin' grand, bitch, and don't you forget it.* Miles had bought the turbocharged model for himself, and that cost another fifteen G's. He now had the two most expensive cars on the street, and that was *just* the way he wanted it. *How do you like me now, dip-shits?*

"Don't get smart."

"And the bounce house only cost a hundred a day to rent. And no security deposit."

Becky stared at him in disbelief. "Are you kidding me? When I was pricing them, the big ones all costs five hundred a day and a thousand security deposit! In *this* county? How'd you get it so cheap?"

Miles loved it when she didn't wear a bra. When he leaned forward next to her, pretending to watch the deliverymen, he pulled half-wood just from peeking down the front of her Milano silk blouse. There were the goods: apple-sized, triangled by tan lines (she spent a lot of time in the backyard pool), and nipples poking out like amaranth-pink Hershey's Kisses. "I'll remind you, my dear, that not only did you marry a man who's wealthy and great in bed but one who is a masterful negotiator." In truth, there was no negotiating. The old guy at the store, Mr. Malpert of Malpert & Son's Party Equipment, gave it to him cheap because a hundred dollars a day was better than no dollars a day, and Miles didn't see anyone standing in line.

"Oh, so that's it, huh?" She kept looking out the window. The workmen—they looked like day laborers—had quickly laid the base and were now unrolling the corner columns and inflating them with an air compressor. She seemed astounded. "Really, I've never seen one that big."

"I know, right? Oh … you mean the bounce house."

"Yeah, Miles. The bounce house." She shook her head, smiling. "At your age, you're supposed to start *losing* interest in sex—"

He slipped over, stood right behind her, pulled out his now three-quarters-hard penis, and pressed it raw against her rump.

"Does it feel like I'm losing interest?"

"Damn it, Miles! I'm not a scratching post!"

"You're not?" And that's when his left hand came around and started playing with her boob, and his right slipped right down the front of her jeans.

"Stop it!"

"Okay. I'm stopping it." He kept doing it. *God, I love this bald pie …* His middle finger angled right into her slit, which started to moisten at once. Then he slid it slowly up and down.

"Mmm," she said. "That's not bad."

"Good. Now pull your pants down so I can give peter some exercise from behind."

She paused, thinking about it.

Miles knew how to read her. Then he started kissing the side of her neck, and that always amped up her mood. "Holy shit," he muttered into her neck. "I have the prettiest wife in the whole world. I'm *so* lucky …"

"Okay, you win," and then she started to unfasten her jeans.

Meanwhile, Miles's cock had graduated to full hardness, and it was beating against the back of her Versace stone-washed jeans and leaving little dark dots on the denim. *Fuck, I can't wait to cum,* Miles thought. And just as Becky began to pull her pants down—

The doorbell rang.

"You gotta be fuckin—" Miles began.

Becky was chuckling. "No nookie today, it looks like. I'll bet it's the bounce house guy. You better go get it."

Fuck! Miles swore in thought. *DOUBLE-fuck!* He stuffed his junk back in his pants, and half-walked, half-limped to the foyer and opened the door.

And now might be an appropriate time for some elucidation as to the sequence of events taking place. The whole of the situation can be rendered as thus: Miles and Becky Bennell, a very well-off married couple living in an up, up-scale neighborhood, were soon to commence with a birthday party for their towheaded, fat, spoiled-brat son named Tommy. It's likely that Miles got that bun in Becky's oven a few months before they'd tied the knot; Tommy had been grunted out of his mother's loins a little less than eight months after she'd officially become Mrs. Bennell. But who gave a shit about stuff like that these days? After that, he'd made damn sure Becky got an IUD because *one* bundle of joy was enough, and he didn't need any more Tommys sliding out of Becky's sausage closet. At first, she'd suggested he use condoms, but … *fuck that!* If a man devoted his love and life to a woman via the institution of wedlock, he sure as *fuck* had the right to dump raw nut into her cooter anytime he wanted—er, at least that's the way Miles saw it, and Becky didn't need much coaxing to go along with it. After all, being the wife of a young, capable millionaire had its benefits …

It has likely been discerned by now that Miles wore his ego like he wore his Diamond/Gold Rolex: he needed *everyone* to see it. That people envied his material position in the world was a matter of great importance to him. In college, over a decade ago, he'd been an insufferable fuck-horn, bragging to his friends at any opportunity about the abundance of attractive women he'd "scored" with, and it might be germane to mention that most of these female conquests were among the best looking in the entire school. Being, 1) handsome, and 2) overflowing with family money, helped Miles quite a bit in this department, but that was beside the point.

And, now, even deep into marriage, his inclination to brag about himself had followed him from college, and his son's birthday party was a perfect example. Seeing to it that little Tommy had a good time was only secondary; the imperative was to throw a birthday party that *blew away* every other neighborhood birthday in recent memory. That meant the best presents, the best caterers, the best clowns, and the best entertainment. Last year, Pete and Janice Cutler (Miles thought of them as the *Cunt*lers) had set up a go-cart track in their huge backyard for their Tastykake-filled sissy-britches son, Mark. That made a big splash, but then a couple months ago, the talk of the town had been the birthday party that Jake Grimaldi had thrown for *his* stuck-up kid, Jimmy. The fucker had rented a twenty-by-twenty bounce house, and those were *real hard* to find. That wouldn't do for Miles, as we've seen—hence his twenty-*five*-by-twenty-five bounce house. He'd also hired a lifeguard for the backyard pool, multiple clowns *and* magicians, and he'd spent a fuckload on presents for *all* the kids, not just Tommy. In a neighborhood full of rich douche-canoes like this, one *had* to stay a step ahead.

Right now, Tommy was at the house of his best friend, Kevin Donovan; he'd spent the night, and Kevin's parents, Jack and Teddi, would be bringing both kids over at one o'clock, the official start-time of the party. A bunch of other spoiled-rotten kids with their parents would show up around the same time.

And now that the stage has been fully set …

Miles answered the door to find, as expected, Mr. Malpert, the bounce house guy, standing opposite him. Malpert was old, grey-bearded, and kind of off-kilter-looking in his round spectacles, old dress slacks, and one of those old-style tweed sports jackets with elbow patches; the guy looked more like a college professor close to the skids.

"Mr. Bennell," he began, "the bounce house is set up and ready to go. It's maintenance free, but let me show you a few things just for your familiarization"

"Sounds good," Miles answered, still pissed that he'd come *this close* to banging Becky bent over the kitchen counter. What a rip-off.

They walked out to the front yard where the bounce house now stood fully inflated and quite grandiose. It had a red base, yellow corner columns, and a blue roof, and was filled with multicolored balloons and beach balls. Heavy nylon screen formed the walls and allowed for the inside to be viewed at all times by vigilant adults. Off to the side sat a tanked air compressor, which Mr. Malpert pointed to and explained, "You needn't worry about that; there's a pressure sensor, so if the pressure gets too low, the compressor kicks on automatically."

"Great," said Miles. Now he was looking across the street where Mrs. London was washing her BMW in the driveway. *Ain't no way that tight-wad hubby of yours'll ever buy you a brand-new Caddy Blackwing like I bought Becky. Wouldn't mind blowing a big peckersnot in your hair, though …* Mrs. London's killer bod was ruined by the asinine curly mohawk hairdo. And the hair was the color of cotton candy.

Only the 2020s would find such a hairstyle normal in high-end suburbia. However, her body from the neck down had provided Miles with some potent "beat-off fodder" on more than one occasion. Beatin' wasn't cheatin'.

Next, Malpert walked Miles to the front of the bounce house itself. "Here's the main pressure panel," he said, opening a lidded box on the side. "It regulates the firmness of the jumping pad." It was a simple apparatus with buttons: low, medium, high. "You can play around with it; the kids like it when you alternate firmness while they're in there."

"Huh? Oh, yeah, sure," Miles muttered, "alternate the firmness," but now he was looking next door where Janet Brill, who looked kind of like Scarlet Johansson but with black hair and bigger tits, was getting her mail. She waved and smiled, then gave a conspiratorial wink. She and Miles had gone to high school together, where she'd been a primo nut-bucket (Janet Brill, not Scarlet Johansson). Miles had fucked the shit out of her on Senior Skip Day and a few more times that summer. *What a wonderful fuck-pig,* he mused now.

"Here are the light switches," Malpert said next, and opened another panel, this one mounted on the front column. "You can adjust the colors and the flasher speed with these knobs. It really looks great at night."

I'll tell ya what really looks great at night, Miles thought. *The smile on my wife's face after I make her cum, and that's what I SHOULD be doing now ...* Several catering trucks pulled up just then, and the staff began wheeling their grills and food carts around to the backyard. Some of the staff were women, and Miles eyeballed them without reservation, thinking, *I'd fuck her, I'd fuck her, I'd take head from her, no way I'd fuck Jobbessa the Hut, but ... well, I'd let her jerk me off, I guess—*

Mr. Malpert cleared his throat to signal Miles's attention. "And one last thing, Mr. Bennell, this metal box down here." He pointed to a metal box mounted near the bottom wooden strut of the bounce house's base. The box had a Master padlock on it. "Inside here is the power coupler. Don't touch it for any reason. If you do, then it can off-calibrate everything and cause a big problem."

"Right," Miles half-heartedly replied. "Don't touch the power coupler—got it."

Just then, the trucks from the petting zoo pulled up, with the handlers leading the animals down the ramps and around to the backyard. A lamb, a baby pig, an alpaca, a pony, etc. Most of the handlers were female, and this just gave Miles more to eyeball. A couple of them were packing some outstanding camel-toe...

"So that's it, Mr. Bennell," Malpert said. "I hope your party is a smashing success. If you have any problems with the bounce house—don't worry, you won't—then call me; I can be here in ten minutes."

"Yeah, right. Thanks very much," Miles said, now watching the picture-perfect asses on the last three girls bringing the animals. *There's an all-you-can-look-at ass buffet if I've ever seen one...*

Becky came outside and called to Miles, "It's time to go pick up the cake, honey."

"Okay, let's go," Miles said. The cake was six feet long, so this would require both of them to go pick it up.

But Becky was staring in almost awe at the bounce house. "Wow! It's even bigger up close."

"I know, right? Oh … you mean the bounce house."

Becky smirked just as her cellphone rang. "Hello?"

Miles was comparing Becky's camel-toe to the caterer's, and Becky, probably ten years older, was easily holding her own. Hopefully, he'd be drawing the end of his boner down that adorable groove before the day was out …

Becky just put away her phone; she looked exasperated. "Damn, that was the bakery. The cake won't be ready for another twenty minutes, they said."

"Well …" Miles got an instant idea. "Let's try out the bounce house for a few minutes before we go get the cake."

Becky's brow rose, then she kicked off her shoes. "What a great idea!"

Miles opened the framed entrance, then said, "Ladies first," so he could get a bird's eye view of Becky's preeminent blue-jeaned ass. *The gift that keeps on giving …*

"I've never been in a bounce house before." Becky chuckled. "How does it work?"

"Simple. You get in and start jumping up and down."

Becky squealed delightedly when she stepped onto the bouncy, inflated floor and started vaulting around. The balloons and balls began to move en masse, and with them, Becky bounced to every corner. Her hair flew up and down with each bounce, and so did her boobs beneath the silk blouse. "This is better than a trampoline!"

Miles somersaulted into the middle of the balloons and started bouncing around himself. Each time his feet hit the cushioned floor, the balloons shot upward. Next, several somersaults in a row, and it seemed like the whole world was upside-down. A couple times he even bounced on his head.

The two of them were laughing out loud when they decided to stop to go get the cake.

"That was a blast!" Becky exclaimed, climbing out of the bounce house.

Miles followed her. "Yeah, but we're not kids anymore. I'm a little dizzy."

"Me too, but—damn—that was fun!"

"Let's get Tommy's cake," Miles said, and

they both walked to his Cadillac. *Damn, I'm feeling kind of weird,* he thought, getting in behind the wheel. He felt kind of prickly and hot, but, of course, he'd just exerted himself. And, what? He felt kind of *icky* in a way he couldn't describe. As he drove down his road, he found himself smirking.

"What's wrong?" Becky asked. Just now her nipples stood out like golf cleats beneath the sheer Milano blouse, and the odd thing was Miles didn't take note of that fact …

"Don't know. I just feel weird …"

"Want me to drive?"

"No, no, I'll be okay. I guess I overdid it, bouncing around in the bounce house like a little kid. I guess all the blood went out of my head for a minute, and it's just now coming back." This sounded reasonable and would explain the headache. But now he thought he felt hot flashes. "What about you?" he asked. "Do you feel okay?"

"I was dizzy for a minute, but now I feel great," and then she did the strangest thing. She reached up and pinched her nipples for a second. "Kind of … horny, if you wanna know the truth. Why couldn't Mr. Malpert have come a little later?" and then she laughed.

But here was more strangeness. Miles had not reacted at all when his wife had admitted she was horny. This was clean contrary to his usual habit.

"Oh, shit," Miles said. "Jack's bringing Tommy and Kevin over at one, and that's about when the other kids will start showing up, but we won't be there yet."

"You're right," Becky agreed. "I better let him know." She whipped out her cell and called Jack's wife, Teddi, who was also Becky's best friend. "Hi, Teddi, it's me. When you, Jack, and the boys get to our house, don't bother knocking, just go in; the door's unlocked, and the maids and caterers are there. Yeah. Tommy's cake isn't ready yet, so we'll be a little late. Just start without us. The petting zoo animals are already there, and the bounce house is ready to go. Okay, see you in a bit." But after the call's termination … she pinched her nipples again and said, "Fuck …"

"What?"

She slid over next him on the big bench seat

and whispered, "I *told* you. I'm horny all of a sudden." She slipped her hand between his legs, which made Miles flinch. "Get your cock out," she whispered hot in to his ear. "Let me suck it …"

Miles's teeth ground. His mood felt skewed. "No, hon. I'm really not in the mood. Later."

Becky was fully taken aback by the response. She stared at him. "Did I hear you right? My husband, Miles Bennell, just said *no* to a blowjob offer?"

Miles saw her point. The idea of turning down a blowjob was beyond fathoming. He'd put his cock in a sack of greased up salamanders if he could. But he just wasn't feeling it right now. "I got a headache, babe—"

Becky rolled her eyes. "That's supposed to be the woman's line." Now she rubbed more intently between his legs. "Come on, pull over at the Hamburger Hamlet. I'll get this crotch-rocket interested." But then she squinted oddly, wedged her hand harder between his legs, then felt around down there. "What the … Did you stuff your cock and balls into your ass-crack?"

"Stop it!" Miles snapped. "I told you, I'm not in the mood! And did I stuff my ... *what?*" And with that, Miles put his hand between his own legs, feeling around. Immediately, he seemed alarmed. He slipped a quick hand down the front of his pants, croaked, "My God ...," then yanked the wheel and pulled into the parking lot of the Hamburger Hamlet, tires squealing.

"Miles, what's wr—"

Frantic, Miles parked, pulled down his pants, and looked between his legs. Then he and Becky both yelled at the same time.

Miles's groin was utterly devoid of any evidence of cock and balls.

"Where's my junk?" he bellowed.

"And look!" Becky exclaimed, pointing down at the barren crotch. "You've got, you've got, you've got ... a *vagina!*"

It was true, and there it was right before his wide-open eyes; the shock was just sinking in. His hands trembled with his realization, and he examined more closely the female sex organ that now occupied the area of space where his cock and balls were supposed to be. The closer he glared, the woozier he felt. *It's a fuckin' PUSSY!* the thought shrieked. *Shaved bald!* He could even feel some stubble. And then something occurred to him, something abstract issuing into his conscience: the pussy. That delectable groove, and the way that bubble-gum pink minora was tucked back behind the lips, and the way the hood looked over the clitoris. "I've got a vagina, all right," he gasped, "and it looks a hell of a lot like—"

"*My* vagina," Becky finished, still staring. "I ought to know what my own vagina looks like, and that's sure as shit it!"

They were both staring down cock-eyed at the vagina between Miles's legs. With all the times he'd licked, fingered, and fucked his wife's pussy, he knew it at a glance. Next, he jerked his gaze right at Becky. "Honey? Why is *your* pussy between *my* legs?"

"How the FUCK do I know?" she yelled back. It certainly wasn't *her* fault. "But wait a minute … If *my* pussy is between *your* legs … what's between *my* legs?"

Miles's lower lip tremored at the question.

"And come to think of it," Becky went on, "something feels a little *tight* down there right now." Very slowly then, she raised her hips off the seat a little and pulled down her designer jeans—

Miles and Becky both yelled at the same time.

There, sprouting awesomely from Becky's bare crotch, was a sizable penis and pair of testicles floating in the crinkled scrotum. This, of course, was disconcerting enough, but more disconcerting was the obvious fact that it was *Miles's* sizable penis, balls, and scrotum.

Miles—ordinarily quite a macho-man—instantly began crying outright, tears flowing down his cheeks.

"For fuck's sake, Miles!" Becky snapped. "This is no time to blubber like a baby! Some serious shit just happened to us, and we gotta find out what it was!"

Miles tried to get control of himself, but then he took another look down at his vagina and started blubbering again.

Becky sat there with her dick out, and she slammed her fists down on the Italian leather upholstery of the bench seat. "What the FUCK!" And then she paused, squeezed her eyes shut, looked down again. "What the FUCK!" She grabbed Miles by the collar and shook him to his senses, or at least tried to. "What caused this, Miles? Something just switched our sex organs! What could it have been?"

Miles brought his hands to his temples, tears still squeezing from his eyes. "I don't know!" he exclaimed, voice quavering. "Global warming?"

"Oh for shit's sake, Miles! How could global warming switch my pussy with your dick?"

"Stop *yelling!*" Miles whined. "You've got me all out of sorts!"

"Oh, *I've* got you out of sorts? But my *pussy* between your legs doesn't? Quit whining like a three-year-old! If it's not global warming, what is it?"

Miles's face was pinkening in distress. "Maybe-maybe … something we ate?"

"That's *ridiculous!*"

"Well, wait a minute. There's that Air Force base on the other side of town—"

"Fuckin' *so what?*"

"I don't know. Maybe they're doing, like, secret government experiments on civilians."

This tamped down some of Becky's ire.

Such things certainly had been heard of. CIA experiments in the '50s? MK Ultra? The Army supposedly putting reagents in the water supply of some town in Texas? "Hmm, yeah. Maybe you've got something there …"

"Or maybe *aliens,*" Miles blurted. "I just read the other day that the Air Force said there might be UFOs for real."

Becky's eyes thinned in contemplation. "I read the same thing. UFOs—yeah, that's a possibility …"

"Or … maybe we're having flashbacks. We did our fair share of acid back in the day. Maybe this is all a hallucination."

Becky grimaced at him, then grabbed his hand and made him grab her cock. "Does that feel like a fuckin' hallucination, ya moron?"

"Stop yelling!" Miles whined again, but when he tried to pull his hand way, she wouldn't let him.

"Keep doing that," she said. "Squeeze it some, play around with it …"

"No!"

Becky continued to manipulate his hand around her cock—er, actually, *his* cock, but between *her* legs. It got hard at once, and from Becky's standpoint, that was a *grand* feeling. "Fuck, that feels good. This is making me horny as a motherfucker," and then she began outright stroking the shaft with his hand and making him cup her balls. "Holy *fuck*. So *this* is what it feels like when a man gets horny. What a fuckin' treat!"

Miles gaped at her. "Becky, what's gotten into you? Since when do you cuss like that?"

She glared. "Since I pulled my fuckin' pants down and found your dick between my legs!"

"It's just not like you to be so profane."

"Can't you focus on the subject? Damn! What are we gonna do? Is it aliens, or government experiments, or what?"

"There's no way to tell," Miles sobbed. "Should we go to the hospital?"

"Oh, right, Miles. We'd be a big hit in the emergency room. What do you think they'd do when they were done laughing? Surgically switch us back?"

"I don't know!"

For the past moments, Becky had kept Miles's hand playing around with her hard-as-a-rock cock. And you know what? It felt a hell of a lot better than when he'd fingered her in the past. "Well, here's one thing I *do* know. I'm hornier than a fuckin' hyena in heat. Drive the goddamn car over there behind the dumpster."

Miles looked over with his lower lip sticking out. "Whuh-why?"

Becky grabbed a handful of his hair and twisted. "Because I fuckin' said so, goddamn it!" And then she kept twisting his hair till he started the car and parked it behind the dumpster.

"Since I've got a fuckin' dick, I'm damn well gonna use it!" Becky pulled her jeans all the way off. The erection bounced up and down like a diving board.

"What are you …?" Miles began.

Then Becky pulled Miles's legs up on the seat, peeled off his pants, spread his legs, and grinned down at his vagina. "I've always wondered how a male orgasm compares to a female's—well, now, I'm gonna find out!"

"No!" Miles meekly rebelled. "I don't want to—"

"Twinkie, cry baby," Becky growled at him.

"With all the times you've stuck this fuckin' thing in me, now *you're* gonna get some!" And with that, Becky expertly spat right smack-dab on Miles's vagina, said, "I'm gonna fuck you till can't see straight, bitch," and slammed that big log of an erection hard into that silly insignificant little vagina.

"Stop it!" Miles cried. "I don't like it! I don't feel good!"

"Shut up, you big steaming Nancy," Becky grunted into Miles's neck. She was pounding away at him, balls-deep with every stoke. It felt mind-bogglingly good, and there was something abstractly satisfying in hearing her balls slap against Miles's taint and just *being inside* him, especially when he didn't want her to be. *Fucker*, she thought. *How's it feel?*

Meanwhile, Miles lay spread-eagled like a bitch underneath his now-cock-wielding wife, and he was taking it hard. The outrage of this *intrusion*, this *physical violation*, left him in a ceaseless state of shock and helplessness. He continued sobbing, pleading, "It hurts, it's too big! Stop it!"

"Okay, I'm stopping it," she mocked. The

sensations building up at her groin were intoxicating and unlike anything she'd known when she had a vagina.

"Fuck! Ugh!" she grunted, driving it home. "Oh, yeah! Shit on a stick, that feels good!" and then she lost all her breath as her orgasm broke. She lay paralyzed within the waves of ecstatic spasms and shimmied at the feel of those big spurts of sperm she was now pumping without relent into her husband's "honey-bucket." One spurt after the next, each one as potent as a mainline of morphine. *I'm filling this bitch right the fuck UP,* she thought in primitive glee, *just like all the thousands of times he filled ME up like I was his own personal fuck-dummy. His own personal cum-container ...* Sweat darkened the full front of her blouse, and then her cheeks billowed at a long, relieving exhale. The bout of animalistic intercourse was over.

Miles lay still beneath her, still blubbering.

Becky lay there, greedily exhausted, but then something clicked in her mind; her eyes popped open as if at an outrageous realization, and then she leaned up and—

smack! smack! smack!

—she unleashed a salvo of hard, vicious slaps back and forth across Miles's face, shouting, "You fuck! You piece of shit! You asshole!"

smack! smack! smack!

Miles lay back in total shock, terrified and shaking all over. "What? What did I do?"

smack! smack! smack!

"You motherFUCKer!" Becky wailed. "I had no idea that a male orgasm was TEN TIMES BETTER than a female's! It's not fucking fair! All these years I've been having pissant orgasms while you were having THAT?"

By now, Miles had all but been slapped senseless. He couldn't even cogitate what she was taking about. He hitched in his chest and stared up watery-eyed. "How could you *do* that, Becky? You-you-you … *raped* me!"

smack!

"We're married, dick-face! It'll be a sad day in American when a woman can't stick her cock into her husband's pussy any time she wants." But then her eyes narrowed as she considered, perhaps, the anomaly of what she'd just said. "Anyway, you've been banging me since the day we met. It pisses me off SO MUCH to know how much better your orgasms were than mine!"

smack!

Miles had to cover his face. "That's not *my* fault!"

"I know, but—"

smack!

"—it still pisses me off royal." She threw him his slacks. "Now put your fuckin' pants back on. We gotta figure out what to do."

Miles dared to cast her a defiant glance. "Well, the least you could do is go down on me …"

Her face turned into a repulsed rictus. "Fuck that shit, man! Yuck! I just filled that pussy up with *cum;* I'm sure as SHIT not gonna put my mouth there!"

"But-but, that's not fair!"

smack!

"Shut your pansy face before I *really* get mad …"

Miles continued crying while Becky hauled her jeans back on.

"Wait a minute," Miles said. "We forgot about the cake—"

"What?"

"Tommy's birthday cake—"

"Are you shitting me, Miles? Our genitals just traded places, and you're worried about a fuckin' *cake?*"

Miles slumped. "It's his birthday, and—"

"That little piglet kid of ours can fuckin' *wait* for his goddamn cake. The fat munchkin'll probably eat the whole thing and not even say thank you. Spoiled little shit. I'll bet he sits to pee."

Miles looked horrified. "That's our *son* you're talking about!"

"Yeah, and he's a Hostess Ho-Ho on two legs who needs a good hard ass-kicking. He probably plays with dolls—"

"Becky!" Miles exclaimed. "What happened to you? You're a horrible person all of a sudden! Did you hear what you just said about our son? Your personality's completely changed!"

Becky gave her stuffed crotch a squeeze. "Yeah, and so has yours. You've turned into a whiny, sissified little girl. Now what are we gonna do?"

"Well, well, I just thought of something," Miles said without much confidence. "Let's say it's a secret government experiment or some kind of alien ray—whatever. Did the same thing happen to other people, or are we the only ones?"

Becky nodded. "Good question. But how do we find out? It's not like we can ask the next guy walking down the street if he's got a pussy."

"Yeah, or stare at girls' crotches and see if there's a bulge—And, holy moly! I just thought of something else. What was the last thing we were doing before we left the house?"

Becky's jaw dropped. "We were jumping up and down in the bounce h—" but just then her phone rang. "Uh, yeah, hi, Teddi. Sorry we're late, but we've, uh, we've got a little problem here—"

"YOU'VE got a problem?" Teddi wailed on the other end of the line. "You won't *believe* what happened! Get back here right away!"

"Why, Teddi? Tell me what happened."

"You have to see it for yourself. Otherwise, you'd never believe me. Kevin and Tommy and a bunch of the other kids all got into the bounce house and, and—"

Becky's eyes bugged through a pause. "Don't

tell me. Their genitals switched?"

Teddi shrieked. "Yes! How could you possibly know?"

"The same thing happened to me and Miles. We're on our way, and don't let anyone else into the bounce house," and when she hung up, she yelled to Miles, "It's the bounce house!"

Miles chewed a nail. "What? You mean the bounce house was what made our genitals trade places?"

"Yes! And the same thing just happened to some of the kids! Now, drive—"

smack!

"—and DON'T drive like a woman!"

* * * *

It was an exclusive manner of pandemonium that awaited them at the house, which was perfectly reasonable given the circumstances. Miles and Becky parked and ran past the empty bounce house, casting it an ominous glance, and then burst into the house. Miles ran with, well, a little bit of a limp, like maybe he had a crushed beer can in each shoe.

A bunch of the kids were outside with the

clowns and magicians or petting the animals—oblivious to the chaos now taking place in the living room where Jack and Teddi had corralled the kids who'd used the bounce house.

"What the fuck, Miles?" came a very harried Jack.

Teddi, a statuesque brunet with killer implants, was just as disoriented as her husband. "They all went into the bounce house, then came out and were … changed! It's just not possible!"

"Tell me about it," Becky griped and pulled down her pants. The big cock hung there—kind of arrogantly, if such a thing is possible—like a mini elephant trunk.

"Wow, there's a bruiser!" Jack laughed.

"It's not funny!" Miles blared. "That's *my* dick! And look what I got—" Miles pulled his jeans down and showed off his shaved pubis and gorgeous vagina.

"Ooo," Jack remarked. "That there's some angel food cake!"

"Shut up, Jack!" Teddi yelled.

Miles and Becky pulled their pants back up.

"So how many kids were affected?" Becky asked.

"Every kid in the room," Teddi informed, "and it happened right after they all piled out of the bounce house. This is fucked up."

Becky's mind was racing, but she found herself fairly distracted by the presence of Teddi, who was looking quite foxy in her knee-high leather boots, denim miniskirt, and chiffon blouse. *Damn, I wouldn't mind putting the blocks to her*, Becky thought. *I'd joggle her fuckin' ovaries …* They'd fooled around in college a few times, drunk, but … *But that was before I had a dick.*

The stray ruminations ended right then, though, when Tommy rushed up to her, teary eyed and lower lip sticking out. "Mommy! My peepee's gone! The bounce house made it go away, and now I have a girl-thing, you know, a cunny."

Cunny? Becky thought. *Is that what little kids call it?* "I know, honey. Do you know who got it?"

Chubby-cheeked Tommy pointed to a blond girl with a ponytail. "Her, I think. Sherri McCoy."

Oh, that little troll. Her parents were perfect cunts. "Sherri, honey? Come here a minute, okay?"

Sniffling, eight-year-old Sherri shuffled over. "I-I-I-I—"

"I know, sweetheart. Lemme see. It's okay, you can show me, okay?"

Sherri pulled her skirt up and Cinderella panties down, and there it was: a bald little cock and scrotum with little balls in it.

Yep, that's Tommy's dick all right. Fuuuuuck me ...

"Why?" sobbed little Sherri. "Why did this happen?

"Because, honey," and then her mind went blank. *Because my fuckin' lame-brained husband HAD to get a fuckin' bounce house, and it turned out to be a FUCKED UP bounce house ...* "Don't you worry, honey. Just leave it to the grown-ups. We'll get everything back to normal—"

"Well you *better*," the little girl snapped, "'cos if you don't, my father'll sue!"

Why you little shit, Becky thought, wishing she could punch the little kid in the face and swing her around by her ponytail. Better yet, she wished she could kick her right in the dick. Now *that* would be fun. "Just ... don't worry.

Mr. Bennell will fix it. Now run along and go watch cartoons," *you smart-mouth little bitch!*

She walked over to where Miles and Jack were standing, listening to the rest of the whining kids whose genitals had been swapped. One kid, Cathy Wheeler, had her pants down and was twirling her limp little weiner around like a propeller. "Look! I'm a plane!"

Jack frowned. "Cathy, put that away, and you there, Mike, is it? Put that candle down."

But Miles was even more bewildered. It looked like a total of ten kids had been transfigured in the bounce house, five boys, five girls. Jack's kid, Kevin, sat on the floor crying, his pants down and his little bald vagina showing just plain as day. "Hey!" Miles shouted, pointing. "Diane, Lisa, stop that right now!"

Both eight-year-olds looked over with shit-eating grins; they'd been rubbing the ends of their penises together.

"This is madness, Miles," Becky marched over to say. "And it's *your* fault."

Miles was outraged. "How is it *my* fault?"

"You're the one who had to get the biggest bounce house just to show off to the neighbors—"

"I didn't know it was all fucked up!"

"Yeah, well, it's *still* your fault. Susie Jenkins was actually jerking off a few minutes ago. How do kids this age even know about that?"

"It's not my fault!"

"Settle down, guys," Jack said. Now the four of them stood in a circle. "I don't see that there's anything we can about this. We need some medical or scientific authority."

"How are you gonna get 'em here?" Becky ventured.

"Yeah," Teddi added, "and what could we tell them that wouldn't sound like a crank call?"

"Well, we better do *something* before the kids go home," Miles said. "Their parents are going to want answers."

Becky nodded with vehemence in her eyes. "Um-hmm. And that little twat Sherri McCoy already said that her father will sue. How do you like that little shit?"

A cast of dread came over Miles's face. "That's just what we need—"

"Not *we*, buster," Becky said. "*You.*"

"That's my loyal wife, all right. I can always

count on her to have my back—"

"Shut up before I dick-spank ya—"

"Come on, you two," Teddi implored. "Quit fighting. We gotta think of something."

Jack was pinching his chin like someone with a goatee. "Did the bounce house come with instructions? Who brought it here?"

"Old guy named Malpert; it was from his company, down in Kenneth City. A couple of day laborers were with him, they set it up. This was the last bounce house Malpert had and …" Now Miles was pinching *his* chin. "Wait a minute! When he was showing me how to work it, he mentioned something about a—damn! What was it?"

"Come on, Miles!" Becky snapped. "Lay off the pot vape! This is important, so remember!"

"Well, I was—damn, I hate it when you can't remember stuff." Miles squeezed his eyes shut. "Malpert was talking, but I got kind of distracted looking at the butts on the girls from the petting zoo—"

"Terrific, Miles," Becky said, frowning. "What a great husband I wound up with, huh? I really picked a winner."

Miles glared. "Well if you don't like it then you can just—"

"What? Leave?" Now Becky stood, hands on hips. "You'd be sitting on the floor sucking your thumb without me. You don't even know how to do laundry."

"Yes, I do … I think …"

"Get it together!" Jack yelled. "Miles! What did this Malpert guy tell you?"

"Something—oh yeah! Something about the power coupler. Said it could mess up the bounce house if I tinkered with it."

"There's our only chance!" Jack said. "Do you know where the power coupler is?"

"Yeah, he showed me; it's on the bottom strut." But then his eyes thinned in some memory. "But it has a padlock on it."

"Do you have any bolt cutters?"

Suddenly Miles looked enthused. "Yeah! There's bolt-cutters somewhere in the garage, I think."

"Teddi," Jack empowered himself, "you and Becky go find the bolt cutters. Miles, you and me'll check out this power coupler."

Both parties split, Miles and Jack heading for

the front door, and Becky and Teddi heading for the hall, but not before Becky ordered the roomful of eight-year-olds, "Kids, don't leave this room till we say so. Then it'll be time for ice cream!"

The kids all cheered.

Becky led Teddi down the hall where the door to the garage was, but just short of it, she stopped and pulled Teddi into one of the spare bedrooms.

"What the—" Teddi made objection. "This isn't the garage."

"Shh." Becky was grinning like a jack-o-lantern. "We'll get the bolt-cutter-thing later. Let's do *this* now." And then she pulled off her jeans. Her cock was already standing up at full mast, throbbing.

Teddi started to make a face of disapproval but then couldn't help but look closer at the big, beautiful boner sticking out from between her friend's legs. "Damn, girl ..."

"Come on," Becky said. "Let's fuck!"

"N-noo."

"I'll betcha this cock is bigger than Jack's ..."

Teddi hitched a chuckle. "Yeah. Like almost

twice as big …"

Becky unbuttoned Teddi's blouse and let her hands frolic over the plenteous breasts, and next she was encircling a big nipple with the tip of her tongue. But when she reached to titillate the area between Teddi's legs, Teddi said, "Becky, no. It doesn't feel right. It would feel like I was cheating on Jack."

"Oh, fuck that hogwash!" Becky frowned. "Not if it's with a *girl*, for shit's sake. If it was with a guy, then that would be cheating, but I'm *not* a guy, I'm just a girl who happens to have a guy's equipment."

Teddi kept looking down at that throbbing, veined cock. Her stomach shimmied just *thinking* what it would feel like going in and out of her. "Well …"

Becky's eyes glittered.

"Okay—"

And that was that.

Becky threw Teddi down on the bed, pushed up her skirt and peeled off her panties, and then proceeded to fuck Teddi like a proverbial two-dollar whore. Teddi tensed up and hissed through her teeth when that big cock slid into her and started banging away.

"Fuck yeah," Becky grunted, then started sucking Teddi's neck. "I'm gonna tune you up, bitch …"

"Oh, oh, shit," Teddi whimpered. "That's so fuckin' good …" She wrapped her arms and legs around Becky's humping body and just let her keep pounding her. Each impact of Becky's groin to Teddi's sounded like somebody slapping raw meat over and over again. Teddi's tongue stuck out, her whole body tensing on and off beneath Becky's coital marauding. "Oh, fuck, yeah, you're hitting rock bottom, Becky! I'm gonna, I'm gonna—"

Teddi came bigtime beneath her hot, sweating friend, spasming hard like someone being electrocuted. But then the marvelous primitive sensations trebled when Becky grabbed Teddi's throat and squeezed hard. Teddi's face started turning pink. Finally, Becky let go, pulled her pulsing cock out, and just jerked it all off on Teddi's pussy, stomach, and bare tits. Becky's eyes rolled back in her head; each big pulse of sperm only heightened the best orgasm she'd ever had in her life.

"For shit's saaaaaake," she muttered, looking down at the huge spattering of cum all over Teddi. "That was some nut …"

Teddi would've been inclined to agree had she been able to talk; instead, she just lay there huffing and puffing. Tiny post-orgasmic twinges flared between her legs like after-notes of some devilish symphony. She was actually drooling.

"Told you I'd tune you up," Becky chuckled, then she grabbed Teddi's hand and used it to smear all that still-warm sperm all over her front. "Does Jack hose you down like that?"

"Oh, fuck him. You just ruined me for life … But wait a minute. Wasn't there something we were supposed to do? Oh, yeah, get the bolt cutters from the garage."

* * * *

Miles and Jack were both on their backs under the base-frame of the bounce house. The housing for the power coupler was easy enough to find, but it seemed that Becky and Teddi were taking their sweet time getting the bolt cutters. Jack, frustrated, was trying and failing to pop the hinges with the screw driver.

"This ain't doing it," Jack said, then he crawled back out and so did Miles.

Where are they? Miles fretted, kind of like a woman might.

"Why don't you go see what's taking them so long?" Jack said.

But the problem was rendered moot a moment later when the two women appeared.

"What took you so long?" Miles asked with some irritation.

Becky roughly shoved the bolt cutters to him. "They were hidden under a pile of junk because *you* never clean the damn garage. Good job, Miles."

"Sorry," Miles peeped.

Jack took the bolt cutters and got back underneath the bounce house. "I'll open this thing or else …"

Miles stood between Becky and Teddi, then something subconscious caused him to sniff. It was a pungent and familiar scent that assailed Miles's nostril. *That's … cum …* It seemed to be coming from Teddi's direction, and next he noticed some dark splotches on Teddi's blouse, like maybe sweat marks. He pulled Becky aside. "Hey, do you smell *cum?*"

Becky grinned back at him, then shot her eyes quickly to Teddi.

"You-you *didn't!*" he whispered. "You *didn't* fuck Teddi!"

Becky whispered back, "I fucked her, and I came all over her—with *your* dick, fucker! And I'm gonna do the same to you if you don't fix this goddamn machine and get all these kids back to normal!"

Oh my God, Miles thought in a lightning bolt of despair. *She cheated on me, sort of,* and he actually brushed a tear out of his eye.

"Hey. Miles," Jack called out. "Get down here and check this out."

Miles slid back under the base. Jack had popped the padlock with no problem and had flipped up the lid to reveal a panel with two buttons on it, each the size of a half-dollar. The first button was red, the second, green.

"Like a traffic light?" Miles ventured. He winced, finding it hard to concentrate because his pussy itched and those hot flashes were back.

"Red," Jack said. "Maybe that means, like, to *stop* the process, a way of reversing it. What do you think?"

Miles was gritting his teeth, scratching between his legs. And he felt ickier still down there from all of Becky's cum dribbling and going tacky. *Damn! How do women stand being women?* And then the most dreadful thought of all struck him. *Am I about to have a period?*

"Miles! You listening? You're in LaLa Land. Come on, man, this is serious."

"Oh, yeah," Miles looked at the panel. Red, green. "I think you're right. The red must mean to stop the process. It's all we've got, so we might as well try."

Then both men crawled back out. "Girls," Jack ordered. "We might have it here. Bring all the kids back out."

In less than a minute, Becky and Teddi were corralling ten whiny, disoriented kids back out to the front yard. The bounce house door was flung open, and Miles said, "Okay, kids! Everybody back in the bounce house! We think we've got a way to get you back to normal!"

The kids all piled back in, all too eager. But

Tommy held back and looked up teary-eyed at Becky. "Mommy, is this gonna make me back to the way I was before?"

"Yes, sweetheart." Then Becky glared a Miles. "Your daddy says it'll work, and you know Daddy. He's always right. Now up you go," and she helped Tommy back into the bounce house.

"What did you tell him *that* for?" Miles exclaimed. "I don't know if it'll work!"

"Well, it better work, because if it doesn't, the poor kid will go through life thinking that his father's a putz and a loser and can't get anything right—"

"But that's not true!" Miles blubbered through a new round of tears.

"Sure it is, numbskull. Because it's *all your fault* …"

"Are we ready out there?" Jack called out.

"Yep," Becky replied. "Let 'er rip."

"Maybe they should jump around," Miles speculated, wiping more tears. "That's what we were doing when *we* changed."

"Finally!" Becky said. "Something *useful* comes out of your mouth. Okay, kids! Start jumping around in the bounce house! It's fun!"

"Here goes nothing," Jack said. There was a loud *click* sound. "I just pushed the red button."

Miles, Becky, and Teddi stood and watched the kids bouncing up and down through the screen. For a bunch of kids who'd just had their genitals switched, they looked to be having a good time. The balloons and beach balls bounced around them alternately. Each time the kids sprang up, the balloons and balls plummeted down.

Miles pulled on Becky's sleeve. He was still crying. "I can't *believe* you cheated on me," he whispered. "You broke my heart—

smack!

Becky gave him a good one across the face. "Stop acting like a blubbering little candy-ass! Be a man, damn it!"

"What?" Teddi looked over and inquired.

"Oh, nothing …"

"How long do we do it for?" Jack asked.

Becky smacked Miles's arm. Hard. "You heard the man! How long?"

Miles's voice quavered. "I-I don't know! Stop being mean!"

"Tits on a bull," Becky muttered. "I guess that's enough time." She opened the side door. "Okay, kids, everybody out!"

When all the kids were standing back in the front yard, Teddi said, "Holy shiiiiiiiiiiiiiit …"

At first, the kids didn't realize something was wrong, but then they started looking around at each other …

Then they started squealing in mind-prolapsing terror.

This time, all their heads had been switched. Tommy's head was now on Sherri McCoy's body.

"Mommy!" Tommy wailed. "Why's my head on Sherri's body?"

"I don't know, honey. Looks like your father screwed up again."

Cathy Wheeler's head was now firmly attached to Mike Newberry's body, and vice versa, and Jimmy Grimaldi's head sat atop Debbie Ross's body, and it went on from there.

"You gotta be shitting me!" Jack said when he stood back up and saw the damage.

"What do we do now?" fretted Teddi.

"But there's still the green button," Miles said.

Did he scratch his pussy again? Yes!

"I guess that's the last resort," Jack moaned. "Okay, kids! One more time! Everybody back into the bounce house!"

Most of the kids did as they were told and were back in the bounce house jumping around. But not Tommy. He hugged Becky around her legs. "Mommy! I don't wanna go back in! Please don't make me!"

Little mamby-pamby fat fairy, Becky thought, then she hoisted Tommy up, heaved him into the bounce house, and slammed the door. *Can't believe I gave birth to that little tinkerbell …*

"They're all in, Jack!"

"Keep your fingers crossed," Jack suggested. Then he pushed the green button.

Becky, Teddi, and Miles stood anxiously aside, eyes fixed on the frenetic movement in the bounce house. The kids bounced up, the balloons fell down. The balloons bounced up, the kids fell down. If anything, it sounded like the kids were squealing in glee.

But in a few moments, those squeals of glee converted to ear-piercing, blood-curdling screams of horror.

"What the fuck?" Becky yelled.

"Something's happening!" Teddi observed. "Get 'em out of there!"

And Miles … well, he scratched his pussy.

It was a pandemonic melee; the kids didn't even wait, they banged the door open and began clamoring over one another to get out of the bounce house and back onto the yard. But when all of them had managed to escape, they all seemed to lay on the grass, kind of twitching and grunting, some still screaming. Becky noted with some disappointment that the highest pitched scream came from Tommy, and there Tommy lay, arms and legs rowing in the air. "Mommy! Daddy! Help me!"

But no help was forthcoming, it seemed. Miles and Becky both stood frozen as statues, staring at the wriggling mass of eight-year-olds, while Jake and Teddi did the same. Then someone broke the dreadful silence and muttered, "This HAS to be the most FUCKED UP thing to ever happen in all of human history …"

And that was probably an accurate assessment.

There was good news, and there was bad news. The good news was that each kid's head had been reattached to the right body … only *backwards.* In other words, the back of his head was now where his face should be. And that was the *good* news.

Here's the *bad* news: each kid's arms and legs had *transposed.* In other words, the arms were where the legs should be, and the legs were sprouting out of the shoulders.

"Oh, man," Teddi muttered, eyes bugging.

Jack added, "Looks like we're *really* in a pickle now …"

Some of the kids were trying to stand up on their feet, which sort of presented a view of someone standing on their head because their *head* was upside-down between their legs. Other kids tried to stand up on their hands because this felt more natural, for their arms branched out of their hips and their heads were right-side up (but backwards). But any serious ambulation failed after only a minute or so of effort, for whether they were walking on their feet or walking on their hands, the skewed positions were too much to reckon with, and balance was impossible to keep.

"The neighbors can't see this shit!" Becky

snapped.

"Yeah," Jack agreed. "We gotta get 'em back in the house!"

"We're going in the house now, kids!" Teddi tried to sound enthused. "Who wants some snacks?"

But by now, the kids didn't give a *fuck* about snacks. They all lay in an apoplectic twitching pile of disarranged arms and legs and backward heads, all sobbing and moaning and blubbering. Especially Tommy.

"Come on!" Jack yelled. "All we can do is grab 'em one at a time and get 'em inside!"

Jack and Miles managed two fucked-up kids apiece, one under each arm, and hobbled them into the house, while Becky grabbed Tommy and Teddi grabbed Kevin. The four kids who remained on the front yard conjured some resourcefulness and walked up to the house on their own on all fours, in a sort of "crab-walk," and it's too bad no one thought to film it on their cellphone because it was one *very unusual sight* to behold and would've made a splash on YouTube.

Back inside, the kids were all herded back

into the living room, and the doors were closed. All four of the adults went *immediately* to the liquor cabinet and chugged some spirits. The kids were all curled up in weird positions on the floor like armadillo bugs, still sobbing in their unfathomable trauma. Would they have to spend the rest of their lives like this? Or could some elaborate surgery offer a remedy?

And what was the exact *reason* for this outrage of physicality?

Tommy falteringly crab-walked over to his parents and looked up at Miles with his backward head. "Daddy? Mommy said you would make us all better, but-but-but-but … you didn't. Why didn't you?"

Aw, fuck … Miles got down on one knee to personally address the really fucked up thing that used to be his son. "I haven't given up yet, Tommy," he began, but, really, what could he say at this point? "You can bet'cha I'll keep trying. And even … even if I can't get you back to normal, I want you to know that I'll always love you …"

Tommy contemplated the words, then his face screwed up, and he started bawling again and crab-walked away.

"Miles does it again," Becky sniped, arms crossed. "Could you maybe think of a more *hopeless* thing to tell a little kid, ya fuckin' empty-headed moron!"

Miles's face turned red, and then he jerked toward Becky as if to pounce. "Get off my back! All you've done is give me grief since this whole thing started! It's not my fault!"

"It *is* your fault!" she cracked back at him. "You just *had* to get a bounce house, didn't you? You just *had* to get the biggest bounce house they make so you can show off to the fuckin' neighbors, huh? What a *dick!* If you hadn't insisted on getting that fuckin' bounce house, we wouldn't be in this mess! No wonder it was so cheap! God damn, I just *knew* I never should've married you—"

"Then why did you!" Miles bellowed back.

"Because you're rich and I didn't wanna work. But you can bet your ass I'll be filing for divorce now!"

With this comment, something in Miles's psyche snapped, kind of like a pencil might, one could suppose. His right hand tightened into a fist, and he raised his arm. "What you need is a good old fashioned knuckle sandwich!"

Becky leaned back and belly laughed. "Miles, if you even *tried* to hit me, I would beat your ass black and blue, and you know I could. Then I'd bang your pussy like you were a roofied bar tramp and make you suck your own dick! So go ahead! Hit me!"

Miles stood there with his fist raised and lower lip sticking out. Then …

His face fell into his hands, and he started crying again.

"See what I get?" Becky mocked. "A regular macho man. But—wait! Here's something we can do!" She grabbed Miles's shoulders and jolted him to get his attention. "Hey! Listen. Where did you first find the bounce house? Was there a rental lot or a place where that old guy did business?"

Miles looked up, sniffling. "Huh?"

smack!

"Where did you rent the fuckin' bounce house!"

"Oh, yeah." Miles gulped and wiped his eyes. "Place in Kenneth City, not far. Called Malpert and Sons."

Becky took command. "Teddi, Jack! You stay here and watch the kids! Me and Miles are going to Malpert and Sons!"

* * * *

They approached Becky's Cadillac. Miles had a horrible stress headache, and what with everything else … "Honey, could you drive? I think I'm too upset—"

"What are you? Mr. Rogers all of a sudden?" Becky spat on the ground. "You're the *man*, so you drive! Get your fuckin' keys out, put 'em in the goddamn ignition, and fuckin' *drive!* If you don't, I'm gonna bend you over the hood and fuck you in front of everyone! All the neighbors will see your pussy!"

Miles whined, wiped his brow, started the car, and was off.

"How long does it take to get there?" Becky barked. She plucked her nipples subconsciously, then rubbed her fat crotch and smiled. "And step on it! You're driving like the little old lady from Pasadena!"

"Stop yelling at me!" Miles sobbed. "I-I can't

concentrate! It's—I don't know—a ten-minute drive, I guess."

Becky nodded. "That's probably enough time," and then she hitched her jeans down and started playing with her big flaccid cock until it got hard. Then she started beating it.

Miles looked over, aghast. "You—You're *not!* You're not doing that *here!*"

"I sure as shit am," she replied, eyes closed, stroking away. "And you can bet your ass I'm not thinking about *you* …"

"Whuh–why not?" asked a now very agitated Miles.

"'Cos you're an obnoxious elitist pig—er, at least you were when you had a dick. Besides, that's just the way it is. Any woman who says she thinks about her husband while she's masturbating is a *liar.*"

Miles made a croaking sound deep in his throat. But he couldn't help side-glancing as his wife gluttonously pursued orgasm with *his* penis. Becky lifted up her blouse, then hitched her pelvis up in the seat, then, "Aw, fuck, shit! Suck my sack, you bitch!" and then she tremored in grips of a raucous orgasm, sperm looping onto her belly in thick ropes. When she was done, she just lay back, grinning. "Fuck, that was good. Ten times better than a girl's orgasm, you bastard."

"It's not my fault!" Miles whined.

"So what? It still makes me wanna kill *all men*." With the edge of her hand, she swiped up most of the sperm off her stomach, then wiped her hand off on Miles's slacks.

"Hey! Don't do that!"

"Shut up," Becky said. She stuffed her dick back in her jeans and refastened them. "Are we there yet?"

Miles didn't think he could take much more. Finally, here was the Malpert & Sons lot, so he pulled right in. Becky jumped right out of the car, but Miles stayed inside, trying to wipe the sperm off with a Kleenex, but it wasn't working very well. *Will Woolite get this out?*

Becky yanked the door open and pulled Miles out. "Come on, shit-head! Don't *make* me break bad on you!"

At the end of the empty lot sat a little building and office. Becky hauled Miles along and banged through the door.

A twerpy-looking guy in his thirties looked up from behind a desk with papers spread out. He looked stressed out. "Sorry, we're closed. All our bounce houses are rented out."

"Yeah, bub, and we rented one of 'em. We need to see Mr. Malpert, and I mean right now."

"I'm Pete Malpert," said the twerp. "The guy you talked to is my father; he got out—"

"Got out?" Miles said. "What do you mean?"

"Did he rent you the big one, the twenty-five by twenty-five job?"

"Yeah!" Becky yelled. "What do you mean he got out?"

"Oh, thank God I found it!" Pete said in a gust of relief. "My father didn't write down the address of the people he rented it to—"

But then a wan voice from some back room called out. "Help! Get me out of here! He's keeping me prisoner!"

Miles and Becky looked at each other, then they both looked at Pete Malpert. "All right, man," Becky said. "What gives?"

Pete's shoulders slumped in some obvious resignation. "If I told you, you wouldn't believe me …"

Becky wagged her finger at him. "Buddy, right now I've got my husband's dick in my pants, and he's got my pussy in his. And back at our house, we've got ten kids with their fuckin' heads on wrong and their legs growing out of their fuckin' *shoulders.* So don't worry about it. I'll believe you!"

"Okay," Pete announced. "You asked for it, so here it comes. My father is, for lack of a better term, a mad scientist. For thirty years, he was a researcher for this top secret place in Virginia called the Air Force Aerial Intelligence Command. You ready for the kicker? They had aliens there, live ones—I'm serious. So naturally, like the good Americans we all are, we tortured the aliens for technological information. But one of the aliens made a deal with my father; it showed my father a blueprint for a machine that could transfigure matter, and the alien said it would give my father that blueprint if my father let it go. So … my father made the deal. He took the blueprint, then let the alien out of its cell, and, well, then he immediately called the MPs, told them about the escape, and the MPs shot and killed the alien."

"Wow," Becky remarked. "Your father's a grade-A prick."

"I know," said Pete. "Now, you would think he would immediately have given that blueprint to the Air Force—"

"But he didn't," Miles guessed. "He kept it for himself."

Pete nodded.

Becky smirked, which was becoming second nature for her since she'd inherited some of Miles's hostile male hormones. "You're telling us that the old guy who rented us the fucked up bounce house is a mad scientist?"

Pete looked her right in the eye. "Yes."

"And with alien blueprints, he made a machine that turned the bounce house into a contraption that switches cocks with cunts, and arms with legs, and heads?"

"Yes," Pete said. "See, I told you you wouldn't believe it."

Becky looked at Miles, tapping her foot. They both thought about it for a moment, then:

"We believe it," they both said.

"It took him years," Pete went on, "to build the power couplers and transfiguration elements.

But eventually, he did, and they worked. However, the process won't work unless the subjects are engaged in rapid simultaneous motion when the element is turned on. So, a bounce house is the most ideal platform; the minute you get in it, you're moving rapidly."

Becky and Miles exchanged glances again. The whole idea sounded like pure bullshit, however: "Okay, we still believe you," Becky said. "But, now, here's the million dollar question. Can the effects of your father's machine be reversed?"

Pete held his hands up. "Of course. Just put anyone afflicted back into the bounce house and push the reset button. Then everything's back to normal."

Becky and Miles *yahoo'd* and hugged each other in a powerful jolt of celebration.

But a question nagged at Miles. "Why on Earth would he rent the bounce house out when he *knew* what would happen to anyone who got in it?"

Pete shrugged. "Because he's got dementia and went insane."

Becky nodded. "Well, that's a good reason,

all right …"

Pete stood up. "Come on, I'll follow you to your house and change everyone back to normal."

All smiles now, Becky and Miles turned toward the office door, but then Miles stopped. "Wait," he said. "What about Mr. Malpert? It kind of seems like he's being held captive against his will."

"Well, that's true to a point," Pete said. "This morning he escaped from his nursing home, then snuck here. When I was gone for lunch, he stepped in and rented you the bounce house."

"Don't believe him!" old Mr. Malpert voiced out to them. "Help! Let me out!"

Miles looked at Becky. "Wow, this sounds more serious than it first seemed. I think we should call the police, right?"

smack!

"You dog-shit for brains, dickless imbecile!" Becky yelled, then grabbed Miles by his collar and *shook* him. "You think I give a *fuck* about some nutty old man locked up in back? Dick-brain! Hammer-head! Back home, we got a living room full of kids with their legs growing out of their fuckin' shoulders! This guy says he can fix 'em, then *that's* the priority, not some nutty-ass old *fuck* locked up in a room. He can *rot* for all I care! *Fuck* him!"

Miles stood shocked at his wife's tirade. "Honey, that's a very hostile attitude. You'll be old someday too, you know. You should have more compassion for the elderly."

"*Fuck* the elderly and *fuck* him! We've got important shit to get done, and here you are harping about some senile nut-job scientist with Alzheimer's! It's old motherfuckers like him who are bankrupting Medicare and Social Security; the government ought to put 'em all in a pile and bulldoze them into the into the fuckin' Grand Canyon!" and then she shoved Miles at the door. "I oughta kick your candy-ass up and down the street! You're a *disgrace* to manhood!" and with that, Miles yet again burst into tears and stumbled toward the car.

* * * *

Back at the house, all normalcy returned for the children. They were all put back in the bounce house, told to jump up and down, and

Pete crawled under the base and showed Jack and Miles the hard-to-see little black button on the side of the panel housing. He pushed it once, and presto! Problem solved! Everybody had the right head, the right genitals, and their arms and legs were in the right places. The kids forgot about their previous quandary rather quickly and soon were milling about with all the other kids, watching the clowns and magicians, playing Frisbee and Nerf Darts, marveling over the animals, doing pony rides, and stuffing their mostly fat faces with the fantastic food the caterers provided.

And with the catastrophe behind them now, naturally, the adults retreated to the liquor bar to indulge in their favorite well-earned drinks. They decided at once not to tell anyone else what happened, and they would reinforce that suggestion to any of the kids who'd been affected. Who would believe such a tale? *They'd think we're all nuts,* Miles realized.

Ordinarily, he was a beer drinker, but right now, loaded up with Becky's hormones, he was not at all hesitant to make himself a milksop, sissified Strawberry Lemonade Vodka Cocktail with a fucking little umbrella in it. *That's damn good!* he told himself. But then a sudden itch impelled him to scratch his pussy again, and that's when it occurred to him: "Holy moly! We were so busy changing the kids back to normal, I completely forgot about me and Becky!"

"You're probably pretty anxious to get Becky's pussy out of your pants," Teddi laughed.

"You ain't kidding!" Miles guffawed. "And I need my pride and joy right back here where it belongs! Let's get out to the bounce house, Becky." But then he looked around and saw no trace of his wife. "Anybody seen where Becky went?"

"She probably went to the bathroom," Jack suggested. "Or maybe she's out back with the kids."

✦

No, at just that moment, Becky was not in the bathroom, nor was she out back with the kids. Instead, she was speeding down the road toward the interstate in her $90,000 Cadillac. The look in her eyes might be described as manically gleeful. By now, Miles had left several messages on her cellphone, and on each one, he sounded a little bit more disconcerted than the previous.

"Honey," she could hear the message on speakerphone. "I'm getting a little worried. Where are you, baby? We need to jump back into the bounce house so I can get my dick back and you can have your vagina. Honey? Honey?"

"Fuck that shit, Miles," Becky whispered to herself and grinned. She turned off her phone and then gave that big package between her legs a deliberate, satisfying squeeze. "If you think you're getting your cock back, don't hold your breath. Oh, and have fun spending the rest of your life with my pussy …"

Who is Edward Lee?

Edward Lee is the author of over 50 horror, fantasy, and sci-fi books, and dozens of short stories. He has also had comic scripts published by DC Comics, Verotik Inc., and Cemetery Dance. A great number of his novels have been reprinted in Germany, Poland, Italy, Romania, Japan, and other countries. He is a Bram Stoker Award Nominee; his Lovecraftian novel INNSWICH HORROR won the 2010 Vincent Price Award for Best Foreign Book (Austria), his novel WHITE TRASH GOTHIC won the 2018 Splatterpunk Award for Best Extreme Horror Novel, and in 2020 Lee won the Splatterpunk Lifetime Achievement Award. In 2009, the movie version of his novella HEADER was released by Synapse Films. He lives in Seminole, Florida.

EDWARD LEE

Printed in Great Britain
by Amazon